MICHAEL J. ROSEN

Three Feet Small

I'm growing!

48
45
42
39
36

27
24
21

9
6
3

ILLUSTRATED BY

VALERI GORBACHEV

GULLIVER BOOKS · HARCOURT, INC.

Orlando   Austin   New York   San Diego   Toronto   London

Requests for permission to make copies of any part
of the work should be mailed to the following address:
Permissions Department, Harcourt, Inc., 6277 Sea Harbor Drive,
Orlando, Florida 32887-6777.

www.HarcourtBooks.com

Gulliver Books is a trademark of Harcourt, Inc., registered
in the United States of America and/or other jurisdictions.

Library of Congress Cataloging-in-Publication Data
Rosen, Michael J., 1954–
Three Feet Small/Michael J. Rosen;
illustrated by Valeri Gorbachev.
p.   cm.
"Gulliver Books."
Summary: A young bear who is frustrated by how small he is
realizes that he has been growing a little bit at a time all along.
[1. Size—Fiction.   2. Growth—Fiction.   3. Bears—Fiction.]
I. Gorbachev, Valeri, ill.   II. Title.
PZ7.R71868Wh   2005
[E]—dc2   2003027495
ISBN 0-15-204938-X

First edition

H G F E D C B A

Manufactured in China

The illustrations in this book were done in pen-and-ink
and watercolors.
The display lettering was created by Georgia Deaver.
The text type was set in ITC Highlander Book.
Color separations by Bright Arts Ltd., Hong Kong
Manufactured by SNP Leefung Holdings Limited, China
This book was printed on totally chlorine-free
Japanese Neptune Matte Art paper.
Production supervision by Pascha Gerlinger
Designed by Linda Lockowitz

For all my big-and-getting-bigger neighbors
at Glenford Elementary School
—M. J. R.

For my daughter, Sasha, and my son, Kostya,
who were little so long ago
—V. G.

I'm little in the middle of everything big.
I'm short and everyone else seems so tall.
I'm under . . . not over. Down low . . . and not high.
But I'm ready for growing and I'm wondering . . . when?
What if I'll always be just three feet small?

My school is for giants. Everything's high.

I still need the step stool when I want a drink.

I can't reach the coat hook, or my hat on the shelf.

I can't touch the floor when I sit at my desk.
I *can't*, and I want to be big so I *can!*

Our kitchen's for grown-ups. I can't see in the sink.
I can't see what's cooking without jumping to peek.
The ice cream's too high in the freezer to reach.

I still need a booster
whenever we eat.

I'm even too small when I go outdoors!
I try to help Dad, but the rake bonks my chin.
I can't push our wheelbarrow.

I can't pull the hose. Even our roses are too tall to smell.
I hate being little. I've been small long enough!

But when Grandpa came over and swung me up high, he told me,
"You're getting too big for this. Next time I visit, you can swing *me*!"
I knew he was kidding, but that made me think:
Am I growing . . . a little but maybe can't tell?

Today when I rode on my tall uncle's shoulders,
we came to a doorway and I had to duck!
If our house didn't shrink, then I'm growing instead!

I went swimming this morning by the deeper-end rope.
When I stood on my toes, my nose wasn't under!

When I dried myself off, I was as long as the towel!
"Hey, look, everybody—there's more me to see!"

My mom took me shopping. I need some new clothes:
I'm on the last hole in my favorite belt.
My ankles poke out of my pajama pants.
My sort-of-new sneakers, they already pinch.
I can't zip my boots that used to be loose. I *have* to be growing.
And wait—there's more proof!

I don't need a grown-up to help swing a bat.
I can pick up a baseball with only one hand.

My dad raised the seat on my two-wheeler bike.
And I'm wearing Mom's helmet,
since my old one's too tight!

Maybe I'm big enough now for a skateboard
like the older kids ride?

I jump on our scale.
I've gained three whole pounds!

And our chart on the wall shows I've grown a whole inch.
I'm taller right now than ever before!
All along, I've been growing . . . but just didn't know?

I'm a little less little, a little more big.
I can't wait for the day when I'm grown like a grown-up. . . .
I'll be BIG in the middle of everything small!

I guess that I'll get there . . . a little at a time.